LOOK AND FIND®

SURF'S UP™

Written by Sandra D. Lawrence
Illustrated by Art Mawhinney

SONY PICTURES
animation

www.sonypictures.com/movies/surfsup/index.html

Published by Louis Weber, C.E.O., Publications International, Ltd.
7373 North Cicero Avenue, Lincolnwood, Illinois 60712

Ground Floor, 59 Gloucester Place, London W1U 8JJ

Customer Service: 1-800-595-8484 or customer_service@pilbooks.com

www.pilbooks.com

p i kids is a registered trademark of Publications International, Ltd.

Look and Find is a registered trademark of Publications International, Ltd., in the United States and in Canada.

Manufactured in China.

8 7 6 5 4 3 2 1

ISBN-13: 978-1-4127-6836-8
ISBN-10: 1-4127-6836-5

pi kids® publications international, ltd.

Drawings of penguin surfing have been around as long as the sport itself. See if you can find these examples that have survived through the annals of history.

Woodblock print

Notebook doodle

Watercolor

Medieval tapestry

Cartoon

Charcoal sketch

Impressionist painting

Cody should be at work packing fish like most of the good citizens of Shiverpool, but he's out on the ocean, practicing some new surf tricks on his ice board. See if you can find these penguins, most of whom are hard at work.

Mrs. Maverick

Grumpy

Freezy

Glen Maverick

Glen's buddy

Sleepy

Cody and Chicken Joe can't believe all the activity on the beach. While Chicken Joe buys all the squid-on-a-stick he can carry, Cody is in awe of all the different penguins who have come to compete. See if you can find these penguins, along with a couple other items on the beach.

This surfer

Sheila's Psychic Tent

Doris' Surf Wax

This surfer

This surfer

This surfer

This surfer

Geek was looking for something specific to help Cody with the fire urchin spine lodged in his foot. Cody got a little nervous when he saw these tools scattered around the hut. See if you can spot them all.

Knife

Chisel

Clamp

Surfboard grinder

Hatchet

Vise grip

Oilcan

Reggie likes to get out before each competition and take a picture with each of the contestants. Who knows if they'll be around after the competition? See if you can spot these surfers waiting for their turn.

Chicken Joe

Tatsuhi Kobayashi

Tank

Doris

Rory

Renato Mendes

Sheila Limberfin

Autographs

While exploring the jungle in search of Cody, Chicken Joe unexpectedly meets some of the natives who quickly invite Joe back for dinner. See if you can spot these members of the tribe.

It turns out that Geek is actually Big Z, and now he and Cody are standing inside his old surf shack. See if you can spot these mementos left by fans in honor of their hero.

This lei

Fan mail

Wood carving

Shell candle

More fan mail

This seashell necklace

Even more fan mail

The day of the huge competition has finally arrived. Surfers and wannabes have come from near and far to be a part of this great event. Scan the crowds on the beach and on the water to see if you can find these characters.

Reggie

Arnold

Cody

Chicken Joe

Big Z

Lani

Mikey

Go back to the surf-art collage and see
if you can find these photographs.

Ridin' the upper deck

Stoked to get the stick
on some epic waves

Acting the kook

"Hi, Mom!"

Catching the pocket

Brand-new longboard

Wassup, Dude?

Shiverpudlians are known for their fishing
abilities. Go back to Shiverpool and see if
you can find these seafood delicacies.

Clam

Blowfish

Octopus

Crab

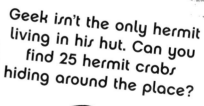
Shark

Squid

When Chicken Joe went off to buy his
squid-on-a-stick, he also bought more
souvenirs than he could carry.
Go back to Pen Gu beach and see if
you can find these special keepsakes.

A tiki mug

A snowglobe

Big Z necklace

Sand pail and shovel

A straw sun hat

Pen Gu Island pen

Geek isn't the only hermit
living in his hut. Can you
find 25 hermit crabs
hiding around the place?

With all these fans swarming the beach hoping to get a glimpse of their favorite surfers, the film crew is having a tough time keeping track of all their equipment. Go back to the beach and see if you can find these missing pieces.

Movie clapboard

Boom microphone

Reel of film

Camera tripod

Light gauge

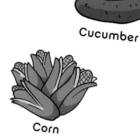
Camera case

Handheld movie camera

Go back to the jungle and see if you can find these ingredients that the natives are using to spice up the meal they're preparing.

Carrots

Cucumber

Corn

Pineapple

Garlic

Potatoes

In his travels to all the different surf competitions, Big Z got to see the world. See if you can find these snapshots taken along the way.

Hot doggin'

Triumphant exit from the surf

Muggin' for the cam

Finishing a gnarly ride

Ridin' a break

Hammin' it up with his board

Head back to the competition on the beach and see if you can spot these items.

Coconut bikini top

Shrimp skewers

Reggie cap

Squid on a stick

Hula skirt

Blue Reggie board

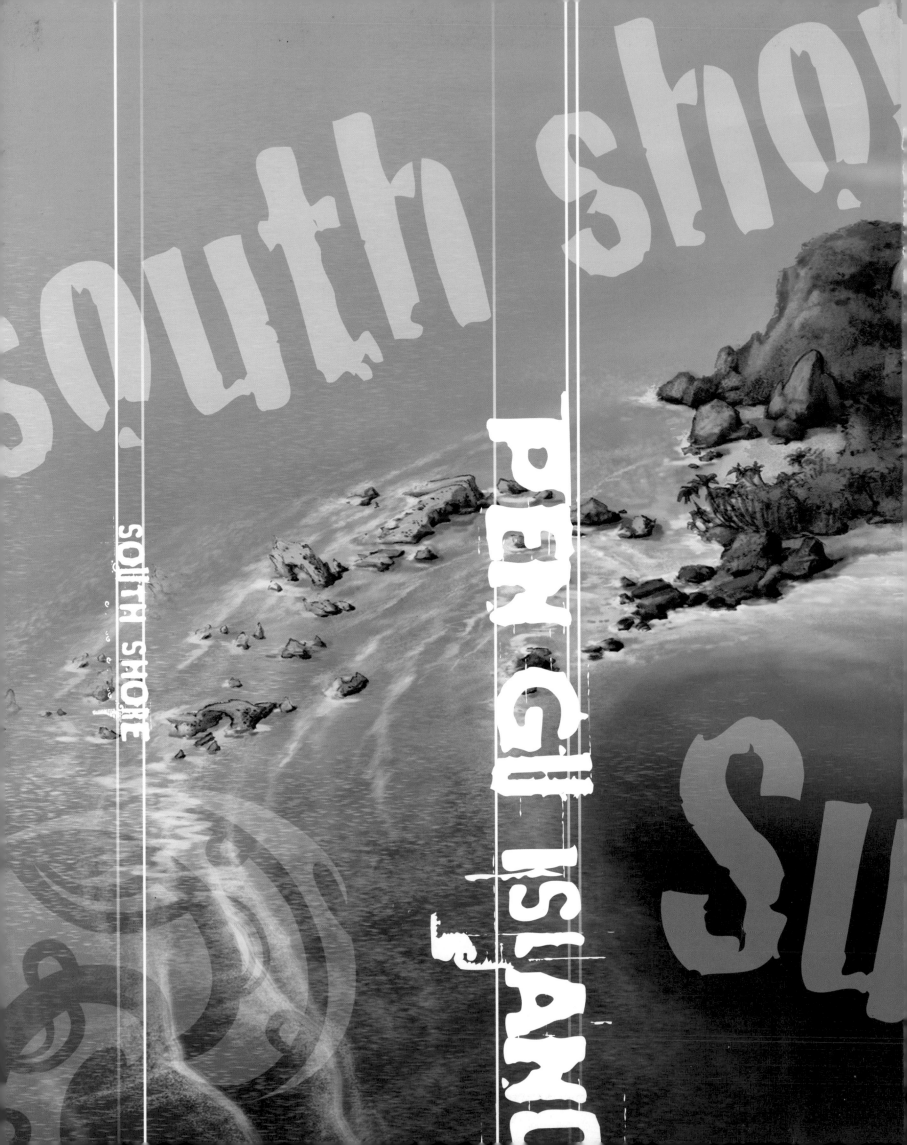